ALMA'S GRACE

A SHORT STORY

ALEXANDRIA BLAELOCK

BlueMere Books
MELBOURNE, AUSTRALIA

Publisher's Note: This is a work of fiction. Names, characters, places, and incidents are a product of the author's imagination. Locations and public names are sometimes used for atmospheric purposes. Any resemblance to actual people, living or dead, or to businesses, companies, events, institutions, or locations is completely coincidental.

Copyright © 2020 Alexandria Blaelock.

All rights reserved. No part of this publication may be reproduced, distributed or transmitted in any form or by any means, including photocopying, recording, or other electronic or mechanical methods, without the prior written permission of the publisher, except in the case of brief quotations embodied in critical reviews and certain other non-commercial uses permitted by copyright law.

For permission requests, please contact enquiries@bluemerebooks.com.

Ordering Information:
Discounts are available on quantity purchases. For details, contact orders@bluemerebooks.com.

Alma's Grace/Alexandria Blaelock
paperback ISBN: 978-1-925749-22-9
digital ISBN: 978-1-925749-23-6

Book Layout © BookDesignTemplates.com

BlueMere Books
www.bluemerebooks.com

ALMA'S GRACE

Alma shifted uncomfortably in her seat.

It wasn't that the white and gold coach was uncomfortable, because it was supremely comfortable given they were flying through the air.

She just felt awkward and out of place.

Partly because the gold was real gold, and partly because even the pure white quarter horses had looked down on her.

Literally and figuratively.

She inhaled the scent of butter-soft leather seats and wondered again, what strange circumstances had led her to a seat in Prince Indulf's coach, flying through the nebulous clouds of ghosts in the night sky.

The sound of the bells on the horse collars was deafening.

Were they to tell people for miles around to get out of the Prince's way, or to keep the ghosts and demons at a distance?

Or simply to prevent gossip in the coach?

Her chaperone seemed entirely at ease, but as a Court Lady, coach rides were probably something she did every other day.

Maybe every day, or several times a day.

Under the guise of stretching, Alma wiped her sweaty palms down her homespun woollen dress, hoping the Lady wouldn't know what she was doing.

Notwithstanding flying coaches, this Royal Protocol thing was a whole other universe.

She'd climbed unassisted into the coach, only aware that she'd erred when she heard the sharp intake of breath and the crisp rustle of skin on silk.

In the real world, if you didn't get there first, you were unlikely to get there at all.

Perhaps it was all to do with the Royals getting the best bits.

Didn't the nobles fight over the rest?

Or was that what Royal largesse was all about?

She sighed. The Lady's poised stillness made her want to fidget.

A lot.

Then something buffeted the coach, and the Lady flinched, grabbed the safety strap and started quietly chanting the Goist prayer for safety.

The woman must be terrified rigid, maybe that was what her poise was all about - too afraid to move.

Perhaps life at Court was more precarious than she'd thought.

Alma leaned towards the window, lifted the blind slightly and looked out.

The night sky was blacker than charcoal, and the stars were like millions of tiny white blossom petals blown by the wind.

And the ghosts?

Well, they were vaguely people-shaped patches of darkness between her and the stars.

Most people can't see ghosts and fear them because of the otherwise inexplicable things that happen.

Doors closing on their own, things falling over and so on.

It's true that ghosts like to stay with their families, after all, they're the people they know and love.

But it's also true that if you don't regularly remind them who they are, they tend to forget they were once living, and covet the lives of those they are around.

Which is how she came to be sitting in Prince Indulf's coach on her way to the palace.

As a Ghost Walker, she could see ghosts, communicate with them and walk among them, coming out unharmed.

Though that meant others often saw her as the cause as well as cure of their ills. And that's why she couldn't stay in any one place too long before being driven out.

So, not too surprising the Prince had heard of her, but quite remarkable that he'd found her.

Alma scratched the back of one leg with her clogged foot and sat back.

When she'd first realised she could see ghosts, it had been exciting, and she'd sought them out and talked to them.

Now they were as ordinary as living people, though to be honest, a bit irritating when they came looking for her.

They generally wanted her to fix up the problems they'd caused when they were living, and it got a bit tedious.

Not to mention that living people often thought she was crazy or a con artist, and it was hard to know which was worse.

Maybe it was the seeming to talk to yourself aspect of it.

And that the dead don't care whether you comb your hair or get a good night's sleep.

The coach started to descend, and she was grateful the bells would soon stop ringing; she couldn't think with all that racket.

Maybe just as well.

With no time to eat or bathe before leaving, and looking again at the elegantly dressed and coiffed Court Lady, she was beginning to feel like a capering monkey in a travelling show.

One of the dressed up ones that did tricks and passed the hat around at the end.

Would they push her in front of the whole court as she was?

Happily no.

Once the coach landed, and she felt and heard the driver jump from the box seat, she leapt (unassisted) from the coach.

Stretching mightily in all directions, she discretely looked around the deserted courtyard.

Well not really deserted, half a dozen or so ghosts were watching on with interest.

They were solid representations of individual people, so she knew their families took good care of them, and they were safe to be with.

She bowed slightly towards them in recognition - it didn't hurt to start off on friendly terms.

The suddenly silent coach clattered away.

The Court Lady abandoned her without a goodbye, leaving her in the custody of a meticulously neat and clean older woman.

Her upright posture, simple and practical white headdress, finely woven green linen kirtle topped by a lightly embroidered pink surcoat suggested some sort of senior servant.

Alma dropped a curtsy just in case.

The woman inspected her closely, walking in a circle around her, "when was the last time you bathed Miss... ?"

"Um, Alma. I'm not exactly sure Ma'am."

"And the last time you ate?"

"Yesterday Ma'am."

The woman frowned, "Becky," she called. A girl scurried from the keep and curtsied, "yes Ma'am."

"I'll be taking Miss Alma to the upper blue room. Please prepare the room and a hot bath. And bring up toiletries and the red and blue dress."

"Yes Ma'am," Becky said and bolted back into the castle.

The girl seemed terrified, and Alma wondered if it was her, the woman, or the ghosts in the courtyard.

The woman looked at her again, and she quailed slightly. "As for you, food first. Follow me please."

Ah. It was probably the woman scaring the girl.

Alma curtsied to her departing back and then ran to catch up.

She thought she heard a ghost snigger.

How could the woman walk so fast while appearing to take a leisurely stroll?

Perhaps she'd learn some useful things while she was here.

A confident bearing and straight-backed speed walk might get her out of all kinds of trouble.

Though it mightn't be as effective when you'd spent the night sleeping under a hedgerow.

Fortunately, the kitchens were down only one short flight of steps from the courtyard, but the shock of the heat and noise made entering seem like descending into hell.

In the chaos, she lost sight of the woman, and it wasn't until a passing ghost pointed her in the right direction that she got her bearings again.

She trotted down the stairs and across the kitchen to catch up, nodding here and there to people and ghosts who stopped what they were doing to look at her.

If she weren't already used to being stared at, it would've been unnerving.

Reaching the woman, and a man who must have been the Cook, she bobbed another curtsy and was grateful to be shown to a table where a large bowl of soup sat steaming next to a big hunk of bread.

She tried to eat slowly, but the soup was delicious, and she was starving.

"Slow down, you'll choke yourself," a ghost said sitting down opposite her.

She nodded and opened her mouth to speak, but the ghost cut her off.

"No no, you eat and listen. My name is Savaric, I was the Cook here. I need you to tell Leofwin the secret of Prince Indulf's favourite chicken is soaking the saffron in wine, not vinegar. And that he doesn't use enough cinnamon."

Alma swallowed, "sure. Saffron in white wine, more cinnamon," though it seemed a strange kind of unfinished business to her.

Savaric smiled and sighed, "thank you. We'll all rest a little easier if the chicken is to the Prince's liking. Mrs Godwaine is bringing him over, so mind you get it right."

The woman was walking across the kitchen with the living cook. "Have you eaten enough Miss Alma?" she asked.

"Yes Ma'am."

"Right, let's get you cleaned up, the Prince is eager to meet you."

Alma stood and asked the man, "are you Leofwin?"

He nodded warily, and she repeated Savarin's instructions. The man's face lit up for a moment, "wine, of course! I'm so stupid."

And then the usual fear and suspicion closed in, but she felt he'd probably try the suggestion.

The chicken seemed to be an issue that needed resolving.

The man bowed slightly to the woman, "Thank you Mrs Godwaine, I'll take care of that for you."

Mrs Godwaine nodded back and beckoned her to follow.

Alma silently followed the woman down corridors and up stairs and was completely lost by the time they arrived in a room larger than any cottage she'd ever stayed in.

The room was, of course, dominated by the bed with blue curtains and covers. But also included a large armoire, a chair set before a dressing table topped with small pots and bottles of things, and an enticingly large cloth-lined metal tub full of steaming hot scented water.

Mrs Godwaine pointed at the tub, and Alma threw modesty aside with her dress and climbed into the tub.

She'd expected the older woman to leave, but instead, she rolled up her sleeves, soaped a scrubbing brush and applied it vigorously to Alma's back.

Alma gritted her teeth but didn't complain. While she couldn't entirely relax in this strange and exotic environment, it was nice to have someone take care of her instead of throwing stones at her.

Mrs Godwaine coughed slightly, "So you're a Ghost Walker then?"

Alma nodded, "Yes Ma'am."

"Isn't it hard to see things that others can't?"

"Yes I suppose, but I'd guess you see a certain amount of things that aren't there too."

Mrs Godwaine snorted, "I hadn't thought of it that way, but I suppose I do. Does it make you uncomfortable?"

"Not the ghosts, they're mostly harmless and generally easily pleased. The living are most often the problem."

"That's certainly true."

Alma twisted to look up at Mrs Godwaine, "Ma'am, do you know why I've been summoned?"

"I'm sorry child, I don't. All I can tell you is that the Prince has been unhappy for some time, and he's looking to you to fix that."

She turned to face forward as Mrs Godwaine filled an empty jug with bathwater and poured it over Alma's head, then lathered her hands and started to scrub Alma's hair.

"Castles are full of tragedy being what they are, and this castle has had its full of tragedy in the last few years.

"Some of the lower staff make signs to ward off curses when they think no one is watching."

Alma let Mrs Godwaine talk as she watched the ghost of an elderly woman in old-fashioned clothing make herself comfortable on the bed.

She seemed to be tutting.

"Mrs Godwaine, did you know an elderly woman in mauve?"

"Sounds like The Late Queen. Why? Is she here?"

"Yes."

Mrs Godwaine stiffened for an instant, then picked up a jug of clean water and poured it over Alma's head.

"Does she want something?"

Alma turned again to look at the older woman. "Well, among other things, she wants to let you know she's grateful for your care."

Mrs Godwaine's lips stiffened for a moment, and a tear ran slowly down her cheek.

"The Queen was a kind mistress, and even though it's been many years, I miss her still. The castle was a happier place when she was alive."

While there were no other ghosts in the room, it was certainly true the castle was wreathed in a miasma of sadness.

The Late Queen's spirit looked pensive for a moment, before shaking herself and standing up to walk away.

Was the castle really cursed?

Mrs Godwaine tapped her lightly on the shoulder, "we're done. You can get out now."

She helped Alma up and out of the bath, before wrapping her in a large towel and rubbing her down.

She pulled a bell-pull, and fairly quickly, a young woman arrived.

"Alma, this is Hilda."

The girl curtsied.

"She'll be doing your hair and helping you dress. I'll be back later when the Prince is ready to see you."

Hilda avoided her eyes while helping her into a linen chemise, so she didn't attempt to engage the girl in conversation.

With the chemise, stockings and light leather slippers in place, Hilda held out a beautiful, but unsettling, lightly embroidered red silk kirtle.

It was clearly too luxurious to be meant for the likes of her to wear.

"Are you sure that's the right dress?" Alma asked.

The girl, continuing to avoid her eyes, nodded.

Alma acquiesced and allowed the girl to pull it over her head. Followed by a blue silk overgown and silver metalwork belt.

She allowed herself to be seated and closed her eyes while the girl combed and braided her hair, topped it with a gauzy veil and silver circlet.

The girl was so quiet Alma didn't notice she'd gone until Mrs Godwaine returned.

"It's time for you to meet the Prince," she examined Alma from several angles, "that's better," she said, "much more appropriate for meeting Princes in."

"But I'm not noble - are you sure these are the right clothes?"

Mrs Godwaine opened the door and gestured for Alma to follow.

"Noble or not, this is what you're wearing tonight."

She closed the door behind them and started walking.

Alma chased her, "but what if I rip or damage them?"

"You'll be wearing torn clothes, so do try to take care of them."

Alma stiffened, "but I'm not ready, I don't know what to say or do for royals."

"It's too late to worry about that now. Just be yourself, and try not to upset him."

Mrs Godwaine knocked on a door, and hearing a murmur from within, opened it and announced "Alma the Ghost Walker, Your Royal Highness," before pushing her through.

The room was about the same size as the one she'd just left, brightly lit by a chandelier of wax candles.

There were shelves of books and papers on the walls, and to one side of the room sat a large table covered by a marquetry map of the world. A bunch of papers and pencils were strewn across its surface.

On the other, a smouldering fire in an open fireplace with a tall and sad well-dressed man standing in front of it.

Remembering her manners she bobbed a curtsy, and he gestured to a nearby low table and two chairs with a tray of cut fruit, two glasses and a flask of wine, "please sit down."

She decided waiting for him to sit was probably ruder than sitting, so she sat, and cradled her hands in her lap to wait.

"You may be wondering why you're here?"

"Er, yes, Your Royal Highness."

"It's about my fiance."

"Ah, as Her late Majesty visited earlier, I thought perhaps your mother."

"Did she?" The Prince came to sit in the other chair, "how is she?"

"Um, she's worried about you, Your Royal Highness."

"Is she, oh dear."

"Yes, Your Royal Highness, she asked me to help you out."

"I miss her too..."

Alma waited for the Prince to continue.

"I'm not sure if you know, but my fiancé died after falling from a tower window."

"No. I'm so sorry Your Royal Highness."

He poured wine into the two glasses, handed her one and took a sip from the other.

It was refreshingly tart.

"I want to understand the circumstances of her death, and that's why I asked you here."

"Oh. Your Royal Highness, I'm not a detective, I just talk to dead people."

"I know. I was hoping you'd speak to Marjery to find out what happened."

"I see. I don't want to get your hopes up Your Royal Highness, but I can only talk to them if they appear to me. If she's happy, she might not come."

"Hmmm," he said, offering her the plate of fruit. She picked up a tiny fork and speared something yellow which was too sweet, and took a sip of wine to cover it.

"I'm sure you'll do your best Miss Alma."

"Perhaps it will help if you show me where she fell from, Your Royal Highness, or let me touch some of her things."

"Well, she fell from the window of the room you're staying in, and you're wearing her clothes. Will that be enough?"

Alma couldn't stop herself from shuddering and hoped the Prince didn't notice.

Funny how it never occurred to the living that the dead wouldn't want to share their belongings.

Hopefully, Lady Marjery was the understanding kind.

"Thank you, Your Royal Highness. I'll do my best."

Alma wasn't sure whether she should withdraw or wait for him to dismiss her, so she stayed put, quietly drinking her wine.

It was a little odd the Prince's private room was so still and silent.

More or less uninhabited by the living Prince let alone anyone else, dead or alive.

Would the gloom lift once he knew what happened?

And how long would it take for her to find out?

After a time, the Prince said, "I suppose I should let you get on with it."

"Of course Your Royal Highness, unless there is something else on your mind?"

He met her eyes for a moment, and suddenly realising she might be seen as too bold, she lowered them.

But he seemed to have made up his mind.

"I am uncertain about what is the best thing to do."

"Do Your Royal Highness?"

"Yes, do. I feel I'm at a crossroads, and everything depends on what I do next."

"That sounds unnerving Your Royal Highness."

"Yes, it is a bit.

"Look, I know it's not the done thing, but just for the moment, could you pretend I'm not a Prince and call me Indulf?"

"Of course Your...," he looked at her accusingly, "Indulf."

If he wanted to be normal, then she'd show him what normal was all about.

She refilled her glass and ignoring his frown, speared something red from the plate.

It was delicious, but not very firm and some fell into her wine as she ate it.

Daring greatly, she propped one foot on the table and crossed her legs at the ankle.

"So Indulf, I'll be gone soon, and it might help, so tell me what it is that's really troubling you."

He seemed to take it well and refilled his glass. Glancing at hers, he smiled faintly and dropped some of the red fruit into it before propping his feet on the table too.

"Well, my father, the King, is ailing, and I'm taking on more of his duties. He's been a good strong King, and I'm afraid I won't measure up to his standards."

"His standards, or the Court's standards, or your people's standards?"

He frowned at his glass as if he'd never considered there might be a difference.

"I'm not sure. I don't want to embarrass him or dilute his legacy."

"They are quite distinct things Indulf.

"Do you think you'd feel the same way if you were the son of the man who shoes the flying horses?"

"I'm not sure I understand."

"Well, shoeing the King's horses must be an awesome responsibility, there's a lot to lose if one throws a shoe or goes lame."

"I guess that's true. A well-shod horse can be the deciding factor of victory or failure."

"Is it possible that's a more awesome responsibility given it rests in the hands of one man, and the King has a team of advisers to help him run the country?"

"I suppose that's true."

"Well, Indulf, I'll leave you to think about that some more.

"Please call for Mrs Godwaine. It's time for me to find Lady Marjery and see what's going on."

She was soon back in the upper blue room, with fresh wine, and next to no idea where to start.

Pouring a glass of wine, she stood at the window looking out at the woodland beyond.

There was a lot to be envious of a Princess for, but at the same time, your life as a Princess wouldn't really belong to you.

In a lot of ways, you'd just be a decorative accessory to the Prince, without many options for passing your time in an enjoyable way.

Assuming you were able to spend any relaxed time with him at all.

Would you be able to sit comfortably with him in the book room?

Would time or the Prince himself be the blockage?

And if you weren't from Court circles, and didn't have any friends, how could you trust anyone to help you?

Especially if you were a poor noble from the countryside, who couldn't afford to buy the things the Court Ladies thought were essential.

And were well aware of how they made spiteful jokes about you when they thought you couldn't hear.

Alma gradually became aware of a faint ghostly figure beside her.

One wearing the same outfit as her.

One that was so weak and afraid it could barely make its presence felt.

It was sad and apologetic but manipulated Alma's thoughts and feelings to explain what had happened.

She'd been so afraid of failing the Prince that she'd been too scared to even try.

In her one act of heroic self-sacrifice, she'd thrown herself from the window to set him free to find a Princess who was strong enough to be the Queen he needed by his side.

Alma couldn't stop her tears from falling.

She'd never felt so sad for a ghost. Poor Marjery's attempt to share her feelings with her fiancé had only made him doubt himself.

It was a mess all right.

Marjery's weak ghost wiped its eyes and smiled with relief.

Alma felt its gratitude as it faded and disappeared forever.

She looked down at the blue surcoat, unsure whether to take the clothes off.

But she'd no idea where her own clothes had disappeared to.

She looked out the window at the lightening sky. Was it too early to call on the Prince to let him know what had happened?

There was a loud knock on the door, and before she could say a word, it burst open, and the Prince crashed through.

In three steps he was picking her up and twirling her around above him.

"I don't know what you've done, but this morning I'm so restless, and the castle feels like it's waking up from a long slumber!"

"Your Royal Highness," she gasped, "please put me down, you're making me dizzy."

He laughed loudly, dropped her to the floor and kissed her on both cheeks.

"I'm sorry, I feel we've languished long enough, and it's time to move on

"I understand, just let me explain what I found out."

He nodded crisply but paced up and down the room as she continued.

"I met Lady Marjery last night. She didn't think she could become the courageous woman you need for your Queen.

"She chose to release you from your arranged marriage, allowing you to choose someone bold enough to be the wife you need."

He stopped by the window and looked out, "so my uncertainty was her trying to tell me to move on."

"That's right, Your Royal Highness."

"Then I will commemorate her passing. She was more decisive than we all thought."

"A good idea, Your Royal Highness."

He turned to face her and bowed, "thank you Alma, you've been a great help to me and the Kingdom. Please consider staying here with us for as long as you want."

She curtsied in return.

"And now I must away," he said, "there are arrangements to make."

He clicked his heels together and bowed again before striding from the room.

Alma closed the door behind him and leaned her back against it to look out the window again.

She wouldn't be a Princess, but could she be the Prince's friend?

What would it be like to live in the castle?

Were there other ghosts she could help?

It might be fun to find out.

THE END

ABOUT THE AUTHOR

Alexandria Blaelock writes stories, some of them for *Ellery Queen's Mystery Magazine* and *Pulphouse Fiction Magazine*. She's also written four self-help books applying business techniques to personal matters like getting dressed, cleaning house, and feeding your friends.

As a recovering Project Manager, she's probably too fond of sticking to plan. She lives in a forest because she enjoys birdsong, the scent of gum leaves and the sun on her face. When not telecommuting to parallel universes from her Melbourne based imagination, she watches K-dramas, talks to animals, and drinks Campari. At the same time.

Discover more at www.alexandriablaelock.com.

OTHER SHORT STORIES BY ALEXANDRIA BLAELOCK

Kiss of Death
Long Weekend in the Snow
Shining Star
Phoenix Child
Ship in a Bottle
Lady of the Looking Glass
Simone Says Hands in the Air
Life in the Security Directorate
Fate in Your Hands
Love in the Security Directorate
Alma's Grace
Payton's Run
The Guardian's Vigil
The Life and Death of Carmelita Basingstoke
Balancing the Book

BOOKS BY ALEXANDRIA BLAELOCK

Stress Free Dinner Parties
Build Your Signature Wardrobe
Holistic Personal Finance
Ms Blaelock's Book of Minimally Viable Housekeeping

Lightning Source UK Ltd.
Milton Keynes UK
UKHW021023210820
368606UK00016B/1103